READY READERS™

STAGE 2 • GRADES 1-3

ISBN-13: 978-0-7607-9667-2
ISBN-10: 0-7607-9667-X

Printed and bound in Canada.

1 3 5 7 9 10 8 6 4 2

BACK PACK BOOKS

Dear Parents:

Children learn to read in stages, and all children develop reading skills at different ages. **Ready Readers**™ were created to promote children's interest in reading and to increase their reading skills. **Ready Readers**™ stories are written on two levels to accommodate children ranging in age from three through eight. These stages are meant to be used only as a guide.

Stage 1: Preschool—Grade 1

Stage 1 stories have short, simple sentences with large type. They are perfect for children who are getting ready to read or are just becoming familiar with reading on their own.

Stage 2: Grades 1—3

Stage 2 stories have longer sentences and are a bit more complex. They are suitable for children who are able to read but still may need help.

All of the **Ready Readers**™ stories are fun, easy-to-follow tales that are colorfully illustrated. Reading will become an exciting adventure. Soon your child will not only be ready, but eager to read.

Educational consultant, Wendy Gelsanliter Dore, M.A.

CONTENTS

Lost At Sea

Written by Frances P. Max
Illustrated by Frank and Carol Hill

Wanda Whale loved to read about faraway places.

"I want to meet new people," she told her mother. "I want to see new places."

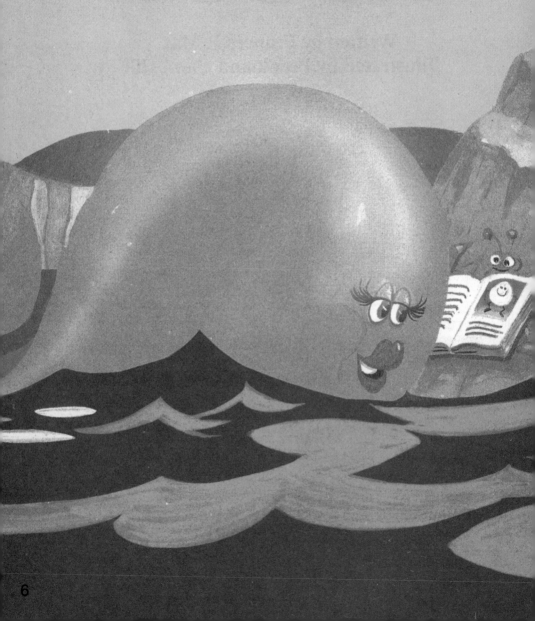

"I'm sure that we can find many new things for you to see," Wanda's mother said. "Let's go for a swim with your father."

Wanda swam behind her parents.
They dove deep into the sea.

First they saw Fred Fish. He was selling junk.

"Do you want to buy anything?" he asked the Whale family.

"No, thank you," Wanda said as she and her parents swam away.

Next, Wanda met Opal Octopus. "I'm riding my tricycle to dance class. Do you want to meet my teacher, Madame Lobster?" Opal asked.

"No, thank you," Wanda said. "I have more new things to see and do."

Nearby, Chris Crab played with a mermaid in the sand. "I am building a sand castle," he said. "Do you want to help?"

"No thank you," Wanda said.

Wanda swam toward beautiful, pink coral. But, when she turned around, she couldn't find her parents. "Oh no!" Wanda cried. "They must not have seen me swim away."

Wanda swam to the shore. But her parents were not there either. She started to cry.

"I can't find my mom and dad," Wanda told her friends.

Gulliver Gull told Wanda to talk
to Sam Clam.
"He can find anything,"
Gulliver said.
So Wanda swam back down to
the bottom of the sea.

Sam Clam was very busy.
There were many fish waiting to
talk to him.

Wanda didn't want to wait.
She wanted to find her parents now!

Wanda was still crying when Gulliver flew by and landed on her back.

"Maybe I can help you with my binoculars," he said.

Then Gulliver jumped up and down. "I see them!" he shouted. "Just keep swimming!"

Wanda was so happy to see her parents that she swam as fast as she could to meet them.

Wanda's father thanked Gulliver for his help. "It has been a long day. We have seen enough new people and new places for one day. Let's swim home," he said.

31

Wanda's parents kept an eye on her all the way home.

SLOW TURTLE
SAVES THE DAY

Written by Agatha Brown
Illustrated by Jo-Ellen Bosson

This is Slow Turtle. He takes his
time everywhere he goes. He often stops
to smell the flowers.

Slow Turtle has many friends.
One of his friends is…

...Gentle Lamb. She likes to chase butterflies.

Gentle Lamb has many friends. One of her friends is...

...Hungry Bear. He likes to eat
and eat and eat.

Hungry Bear has many friends
too. One friend is...

...Proud Peacock.

He likes to show off his beautiful feathers.

Slow Turtle, Gentle Lamb, Hungry Bear and Proud Peacock are all good friends. Sometimes they play together.

One day, Proud Peacock got his tail stuck in a bush. Everyone helped to get him out. The friends always help each other.

One Sunday at noon the four friends planned to give another friend, Busy Beaver, a medal. They wanted to honor him for building his dam all by himself.

But Hungry Bear did not think that Slow Turtle would make it to the big meadow on time.

"I hope that you can move faster or you will miss the whole thing," Hungry Bear said to Slow Turtle.

Slow Turtle was sad. He wanted to be there for Busy Beaver.

The next day, Slow Turtle
worked out.

He crawled to the left.

He crawled to the right.

He crawled to the left and right
as fast as he could.

On Sunday, Hungry
Bear took off for the Big
Meadow. He had his bat so
that he could play ball
on the way. He also had
Beaver's medal.

"I hope that you make
it," he said to Slow Turtle.

"I will! I will!" Slow
Turtle said.

But Slow Turtle could not help himself.

He stopped to smell the flowers.

He stopped to say hello to a busy ant.

He stopped to look at a mushroom.

That's when he found a round and shiny medal hanging on a blue ribbon.

Slow Turtle put the medal around his neck. Then he went left and right and left again as fast as he could to the Big Meadow.

When Slow Turtle got to the Big Meadow, his friends were looking everywhere for the lost medal.

"Hooray!" they shouted when they saw Slow Turtle. "You found Busy Beaver's medal!"

"I was running so fast that I didn't know I lost it," Hungry Bear said.

"Sometimes it is good to take your time," Slow Turtle said.

"You are so right," Hungry Bear said. "You saved the day, Slow Turtle!"

Slow Turtle was proud!

No Snow for Seth

Written by Jean Davis Callaghan
Illustrated by Mikke Wotton

"Why is the snow melting?"
Seth asks his mother.

"Winter is over," says Mother, "until next year."

Seth plays outside in the snow all day.

He gets an idea.
He puts some snow in a big jar.

He puts the jar of snow
into the freezer.

Now Seth has snow to play with all year round.

He makes snowballs,
and snow houses.

He makes little snowmen.

"It's warm today," says Mother.
"How about coming outside
with me?"

"No, thank you," says Seth. "I will stay inside and play with my snow."

Seth wonders, "What could
Mother be doing out there?"
He runs outside to see.

Mother is working in the garden.
"The seeds you planted grew
into flowers!" Seth cries.

Seth helps Mother tend
the flowers.

"Oh, no! My snow!" Seth cries.
"I left the jar on the table!"
He runs back inside.

The snow has melted.
Now it is just water.

"The flowers need water,"
Mother says.

Seth pours some of the water
onto the flowers.

Then he pours some onto his toes!

It feels nice and cool.

"I have fun in the winter,"
says Seth.
"And now I'll have fun
in the spring!"

Rosie's Two Left Feet

Written by Jean Davis Callaghan
Illustrated by Florie Freshman

It is Grandpa's birthday.
Rosie and her family
are going to his party.

"Here are your new party shoes," Mother says.

Rosie is happy about going to a grown-up party, and about having new party shoes.

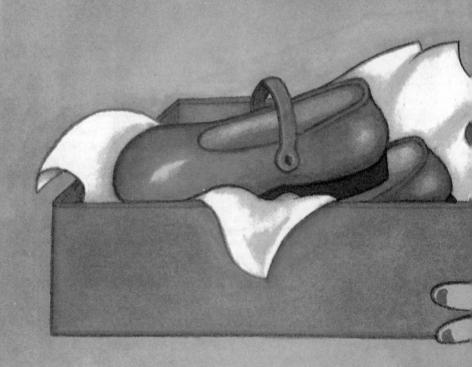

95

Rosie and her sister, Anne,
finish getting ready.

"My new shoes feel funny,"
Rosie says.

"Oh, dear," says Mother.
"The store gave us two
left-foot shoes.
We will have to return them
in the morning."

Perhaps school shoes will look nice with Rosie's party dress. No, they don't.

How about sneakers?
Where are they?

"Those sneakers don't look very nice with your party dress, either," says Mother.

Anne has an idea!

She shines her old party shoes
that she has outgrown.

Anne saves the day!

Her old shoes look
brand-new again.
So clean.
Such shiny buckles.

"Thank you, Anne," says Rosie.
Rosie is so proud.

Anne even finds a ribbon
to match the shoes.

Now everyone can
go to the party.

Happy birthday, Grandpa!

Duffy Takes a Dip

Written by Jean Davis Callaghan
Illustrated by Joan Thoubboron

"Good morning, Mama and Papa," the seven ducklings say.

"Good morning, ducklings."

"Today I will teach you how to swim," says Mama. "Come, follow me."

Duffy would rather play
on the shore.

"Come along, Duffy," says Mama.

"Try to do what I do,"
Mama tells the ducklings.

All the ducklings try—
except Duffy.

His brothers and sisters call,
"Look, Duffy!"

"Watch this!"

"Can you do this, Duffy?" they ask.

"One, two, three, four, five, six ducklings," Papa counts. "Where's Duffy?"

Papa finds Duffy hiding
on the shore.
"I'm afraid of the water,"
Duffy says.

"When I was young, I was afraid of the water, too," Papa tells him.

Papa takes Duffy for a ride
on his back.

"Oh, this is fun!" says Duffy.

"Look at the fish, Papa!"

"The water feels good!"
Duffy says.

"And it's fun to splash!"

"Papa," Duffy laughs,
"I can see myself!"

Soon Duffy is swimming
all by himself.
"Wheeeee!"

Patty
for President

Written by Jean Davis Callaghan
Illustrated by Mary Ann Fraser

Pam and Patty are twins.

They are in the second grade.

Friday, the class will vote for the class president.

"Who will you vote for?"
Pam asks Patty.

"For myself," says Patty.
"I want to be president."

Patty tells everyone,
"Vote for me
for president."

Bossy Patty tells Pam,
"I want you to be my helper.
Go get some cookies
and pass them out.
Say they are from me."

"Also, I want you to help everyone with their homework, and tell them it was my idea."

Pam doesn't like being bossed around, but she does love her sister.

So she bakes cookies and
hands them out to the class.

The class likes the cookies
so much, Patty asks Pam
to bring them every day.

During recess, and after school,
Pam helps the other students
with their homework.

It bothers Pam that Patty
is so bossy, but Pam keeps
working hard for her sister.

Pam works so hard that
she gets tired.
One day, she almost
falls asleep in class.

Patty doesn't do any work.
She only sits on the swing,
talking and laughing—

and eating the cookies
that Pam made.

At last it is Friday.

The teacher says, "It's time
for the class to vote."

Everyone waits to see who will get the most votes.

The teacher says, "The class president is…

…Pam!"

Pam wins because the class thinks she is a kind person, and a hard worker.

Sebastian's Good Idea

Written by Jean Davis Callaghan
Illustrated by Joe Messerli

Sebastian Squirrel is
busy working.
He is looking for acorns.

His friends are busy playing.
They are having fun.

It is important to gather acorns
for the winter.
But it is also important to play.

"Come play," Sebastian's friends call.

"Not now," Sebastian answers.
"I have to fill my acorn basket."

Sebastian finds acorns under
the trees while his friends
swing from tree to tree.

Sebastian brings the acorns
to his house...

...while his friends play
hide and seek.

Sebastian's home is almost filled with acorns.

Now he is ready for fun.

"Let's play with my new ball!"
shouts Sebastian.
But where are Sebastian's friends?

They're not playing anymore.

Now they are busy gathering
acorns.

Sebastian plays by himself while his friends gather acorns.

At last, Sebastian's friends
are finished working.

Their homes are filled
with acorns, too.

But now it is too late to play.

It's time for Sebastian and his
friends to go home for dinner.

"Tomorrow, let's all gather acorns together," Sebastian says.
"And then we can play together, too."

"What a good idea!" his friends agree as they head home.

BIRTHDAY SURPRISE

Written by Joanie Geist
Illustrated by M. Cambraia Magalhaes

Blue-Ribbon Bunny was taking his morning hop when he came across Mother Hen's orphans.

"Guess what!" Skippy Squirrel said. "It's my birthday!"

"The birthday breakfast is ready," Mother Hen shouted to her charges.

"What's that?" Blue-Ribbon Bunny asked.

"I can't afford a big birthday party," she said, "so I make up for it with a small treat at breakfast."

The next day, deep in thought, Blue-Ribbon Bunny ran into Old Skunk.

"Old Skunk," Blue-Ribbon Bunny asked, "did you have birthday parties when you were little?"

"Yes," Skunk said, "birthday parties are my happiest memories."

"Mine too," Blue-Ribbon Bunny said as he waved goodbye.

Along the road, he smelled something wonderful.

Sophie Squirrel was baking pies.

"Sophie," Blue-Ribbon Bunny asked, "did you have birthday parties when you were little?"

"Of course," Sophie said. "Why do you ask?"

Blue-Ribbon Bunny told her about the orphans. "What do you think about all of the village grown-ups throwing a birthday party for the kids?" he asked.

The next morning, Sophie sent
Blue-Ribbon Bunny a note.

"You had a good idea," the note
read. "I want to help the orphans too.
Let's give them a surprise birthday
party! I'll do the baking."

Blue-Ribbon Bunny called his friend, Barney Bird.

"Tell everyone to gather at the clearing on the day after tomorrow," he said.

Soon, everyone in town knew about the party.

Meanwhile, Sophie baked up a storm. Pies and cakes filled her cottage. Blue-Ribbon Bunny stopped by to see how things were going.

"You can be my official taste-tester," Sophie said.

Blue-Ribbon Bunny didn't mind a bit.

In the afternoon, Blue-Ribbon
Bunny went to see the toy-maker,
Webster Woodchuck.

"I'll make some toys," Webster said.
"I'll start right away."

As the big day dawned, Sophie
worked harder than ever. A parade of
neighbors helped deliver the goodies.

The clearing buzzed with activity. Sophie brought the cakes and set the table. Everything was ready.

Blue-Ribbon Bunny gathered the guests of honor. "Hurry," he said, "Mother Hen wants you in the clearing at once."

"Surprise!" the grown-ups shouted
when the children arrived. "Happy
Birthday!"

"Hooray!" the happy children shouted, munching the goodies.

The woods had never seen such a feast! It lasted right up until the children's bedtime. Then the grown-ups sat at the table and ate.

After the party, Sophie headed home. She was very happy that the orphans had so much fun.

"Hmm," she said to herself, "maybe I'll bake a cake and throw another surprise party – for a kind bunny."

And that is just what she did.

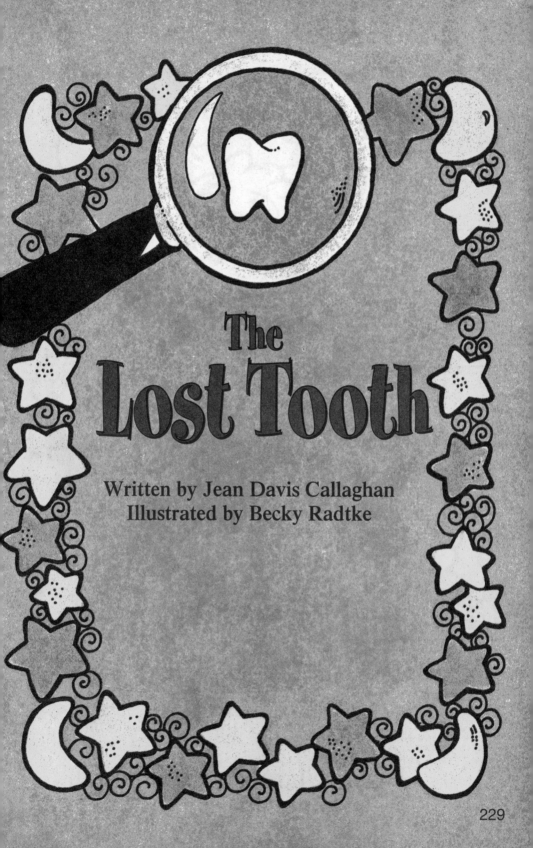

The Lost Tooth

Written by Jean Davis Callaghan
Illustrated by Becky Radtke

Today Clarence lost a tooth.

It fell right out of his mouth.

He is so happy.

Clarence runs all over the house
to find his sister, Terri.

He tells Terri all about the
Tooth Fairy.

235

Maybe Clarence should put the tooth under his pillow now.

But the tooth is gone!

Now he has lost the tooth twice!

"I have to find it," Clarence says.

He looks all over the house.

Did it fall down the drain in the sink?

Did it fall under his bed?

No, it's not there.

Maybe Clarence dropped the tooth
while he was feeding the fish.

No, it's not in the aquarium.

Just then, Terri yells, "Clarence! I found it!"

Clarence runs through the house.

There's the tooth.

Terri found it right
behind the vase on the
kitchen table.

Clarence is so happy.

He gives Terri a big hug.

Now the Tooth Fairy will come
and leave Clarence money for
the tooth under his pillow.

What a fun night this will be!

Clarence will buy something
good with his tooth money.

He will buy ice cream to share
with Terri.

A Day at the CARNIVAL

Written by Andrea Bear
Illustrated by M. Cambraia Magalhaes

The carnival is in town!
During the day, people play.

But when the carnival closes,
the stuffed animals have their say.

Rabbit, Frog, Mouse, and Elephant couldn't wait to go on all the rides.

"Let's try every ride and vote on
which one is the best," Rabbit said.

The four friends ran to the
race track.

"Beep! Beep!" Mouse said.
"Driving is fun. This is the best ride!"

"Let's go on the Ferris wheel,"
Frog said.

The friends each got a seat on
the tall Ferris wheel.

"You can see the whole town from up here," Elephant said. "This is the best ride!"

Frog looked all around the carnival. "Let's go on the airplane ride," he said.

Everyone screamed as the planes went higher and higher into the air.

"Whee! Flying is fun," Frog
said. "This is the best ride!"

"Let's go on the Merry-Go-Round," Rabbit said.

Everyone laughed as their horses

went up and down.

"I like how my long ears flew back as the Merry-Go-Round went around and around," Rabbit said. "This is the best ride!"

"We all think a different ride is the best one," Mouse said. "How can we pick just one?"

The four friends looked at each other. "Let's go on everything again!" they shouted.

And they did.